D1643641

Humphrey's

Mummy

me

Daddy Lottie Baby Jack

Family ♥

Sally Hunter

PUFFIN BOOKS

20091563

MORAY COUNCIL
LIBRARIES &
INFORMATION SERVICES

JA

This is Humphrey. ♡

Humphrey loves everyone
in his family.

Here is Lottie, Humphrey's big sister.

Lottie likes cooking dinner for her babies

... being teacher

(but she is a bit bossy sometimes!)

...going out to parties

and making magic wishes come true.

Here is Baby Jack, Humphrey's little brother.

Baby Jack's favourite toy is Dog.

Dog used to bark but the string broke.

Baby Jack always talks baby talk.

He dribbles quite a lot too...

Baby Jack likes joining in

... but he can't really play properly
(because he is too young to understand).

Here are Humphrey's mummy and daddy.

Humphrey thinks Mummy and Daddy
are sometimes a bit silly...

which isn't right really because
they are supposed to be grown-ups.

Mummy is very good at playing

and she comes to tea when it is
one of the babies' birthdays.

But Mummy always tells
Humphrey to tidy his bedroom.
Humphrey likes his bedroom all messy.

If Daddy gets home before bedtime...

he is the train driver and
Humphrey is the guard.

Daddy is a very good horsey too!

Here are Humphrey's granny and grandad.

Most Sundays, Humphrey goes to tea.
Granny makes cherry cakes
because they are his favourite.

Grandad usually digs the garden.

Humphrey is always a very big help...

Then Humphrey, mop, Lottie and her babies.

Daddy, Mummy, Baby Jack and Dog ...

all go home to the old house at the top of the hill.

For My Dad
Love You
Sal x

PUFFIN BOOKS

Published by the Penguin Group:
London, New York, Australia, Canada, India, New Zealand and South Africa
Penguin Books Ltd, Registered Offices: 80 Strand, London WC2R 0RL, England

www.penguin.com

First published 2002

1 3 5 7 9 10 8 6 4 2

Copyright © Sally Hunter, 2002

All rights reserved

The moral right of the author/illustrator has been asserted

Made and printed in Singapore by Tien Wah Press (Pte) Ltd

ISBN 0-670-91380-4

To find out more about Humphrey's world, visit the web site at www.humphreys-corner.com